KAY THOMPSON'S ELOISE

Eloise's New Bonnet

STORY BY **Lisa McClatchy**

ILLUSTRATED BY **Tammie Lyon**

Ready-to-Read

Simon Spotlight

New York   London   Toronto   Sydney   New Delhi

SIMON SPOTLIGHT

An imprint of Simon & Schuster Children's Publishing Division

1230 Avenue of the Americas, New York, NY 10020

Copyright © 2007 by the Estate of Kay Thompson

Manufactured in China 0815 LEO

I am Eloise.
I am six.
I live in The Plaza hotel
on the tippy-top floor.

I have a dog.
His name is Weenie.

Here is what I like to do:
put sunglasses on Weenie.

Today the sun is shining.
Spring has sprung.
I put my sunglasses on too.

Nanny says, "Eloise,
you need a new hat."

Lampshades make very good hats.

"No, no, no, Eloise," Nanny says. "You need to find a real hat."

"I know where to find
a real hat," I say.
"I will visit the kitchen."

Chef's hat makes
a very good hat.

"I know," I say. "I
will visit room service."

Room service hats
make very good hats.

"No, no, no, Eloise,"
Nanny says.
"That hat has no brim."

"Hmm," I say.
"I will visit
    the bell captain!"

Bell captain hats
make very good hats.

"No, no, no, Eloise," Nanny says. "We need a hat that is a pretty color."

I visit the lobby.
There are hats everywhere!

I try on a lady's hat.
It is a pretty color,
and it has a bird on top.
"Perfect," I say.

Nanny and the manager
do not agree.

"Please give the lady
her hat back,"
Nanny says.

"Sorry."

"Eloise, I have a surprise,"
Nanny says.
She hands me a box.

Inside is a new hat
just for me.

Oh, I love, love, love hats!